Treasure's Adventures
Five Tiny Tales

by Robin Epstein
Illustrated by the Disney Storybook Art Team

DISNEP PRESS
Los Angeles · New York

Editorial by Eric Geron
Design by Lindsay Broderick
All rights reserved. Published by Disney Press, an imprint of Disney Book Group.
No part of this book may be reproduced or transmitted in any form or by any means,
electronic or mechanical, including photocopying, recording, or by any information
storage and retrieval system, without written permission from the publisher.

For information address Disney Press, 1101 Flower Street, Glendale, California 91201.

Printed in China
First Hardcover Edition, April 2016
Library of Congress Control Number: 2015948745
1 3 5 7 9 10 8 6 4 2
ISBN 978-1-4847-4648-6
FAC-025393-16029

For more Disney Press fun, visit www.disneybooks.com

Download the Whisker Haven Tales App

Welcome to Whisker Haven, dear!

I'm **Ms. Featherbon**, the hummingbird fairy and gatekeeper of Whisker Haven—and, from time to time, a party planner! I have so many wonderful places to show you . . . the **Pawlace**, **Whisker Haven Village**, **Whisker Woods**, **Whisker Sea**, and so much more. I manage this peaceful kingdom with help from all of the **Palace Pets**—Treasure, Petite, **Sultan**, Pumpkin, **Berry**, and Dreamy, to name a few. All those who reside in Whisker Haven cherish the **beauty of kindness**, the **glamour of helping others**, and, of course, the **royal heart of friendship**. . . .

Splendificent adventures await you in Whisker Haven!

Whisker Haven

Whisker Sea

Pawlace

Contents

Treasure Hunt

"**All** paws and hooves on deck!" called Ms. Featherbon.

The blue hummingbird fairy and gatekeeper to **Whisker Haven** flew out of the **Pawlace** and zipped across the Whisker Haven sky. "Dearie-dearest me!" she exclaimed. "What an incredible day we have ahead of us!" Her wings flapped so fast that her hat nearly blew off. "Oh-my-oh-me-oh-my! **There's so much to do! So very, very much to do!**"

She hovered over **Whisker Haven Village**, a quaint town full of shops and homes of the **Critterzens**. "Critterzens, your attention!" said Ms. Featherbon. "Meeting in Whisker Woods! **Meeting in Whisker Woods!**" She flew over to the beautifully lush woods and landed on a tree branch overlooking a large and sunny clearing.

Soon enough, the Critterzens had crowded into the clearing before her, followed by the **Palace Pets**—Petite the yellow pony, with pink tail and mane; **Berry** the bunny, with blue fur and fluffy white tail; Pumpkin the white puppy; and Sultan the tiger. As an eager buzzing began to build, Ms. Featherbon held up one of her wings.

"Hello, friends," she said. "What was I going to say . . . Ah, yes! Tonight is the Glitter Ball! A royally enchanting evening awaits us!"

The crowd cheered.

Ms. Featherbon unrolled a sheet of parchment and read: "'For the opening of the Glitter Ball, magic from the Glitterbits shall light up the night sky.'" She smiled at her friends.

"A splendificent display of Glitterworks shall shower down upon you, and you shall sparkle as you dance!"

"This is going to be the most glamorous dance party ever!" said Pumpkin.

"Woo-hoo! I can't wait to rock and roar!" said Sultan.

"We're going to have so much fun tonight!" said Berry. "It's going to be **berry sweet**!"

"The Glitter Ball rules!" said Petite. "Speaking of rules, where's my rule book?"

"I'm so glad you're all here!" Ms. Featherbon said. She surveyed the crowd of Palace Pets and Critterzens. "Well, I'll be humdinged!" she said. "I

14

don't see Dreamy. Where's Dreamy?"

"I didn't see Dreamy, but I heard her," Berry said, perking up her long bunny ears. "And it sounded a little like this: ZZZ-Zzzz-ZZZ-hoohhh-pupuhpuh-zzZZzz . . ."

"Translation," Petite said, pulling out a manual called *Snores and What They Mean*. "'I'm getting my beauty sleep.'"

"Napping is important," said Ms. Featherbon, "so we'll let her sleep." Her wings twitched. "But I need everyone else's paws and hooves on deck!"

"What can we do to help?" asked Mr. Chow, the silvery blue cat in a hat and apron.

"You can be in charge of preparing all of your **finest kibbles**," said Ms. Featherbon.

Mr. Chow nodded. "I'd love nothing more than to prepare all sorts of special kibbles for the ball."

"Royally wonderful!" said Ms. Featherbon. She turned to **Lucy**, the sweet brown dog in a yellow dress. "Lucy, can you gather up all your **squeakiest squeak balls**?"

"Yes! You got it!" said Lucy.

Ms. Featherbon faced **Tillie**, the orange-and-peach-colored cat with tutus on her head and waist. "Tillie, can you please **make sure everyone is dressed just right** for the Glitter Ball?"

"Tutu tailor at your service," Tillie said.

"How simply marvelous!" said Ms. Featherbon. "My Glitterbits will enchant everything to make the Glitter Ball **sparkle**! Now, as for everyone else, I've pecked your tasks on the Glitter Ball to-do list hanging on this tree." She gestured to the trunk of the tree where she was perched.

Everyone nodded as they read from the list.

Berry hopped up and down. **"I get to help Mr. Chow select all his kibbles!"**

"I'm going to help Lucy pick out the squeakiest squeak balls!" said Sultan.

"And Petite and I are going to help Tillie make sure everyone is dressed in their very best!" said Pumpkin, twirling.

"Splendificent!" said Ms. Featherbon. "We want tonight to be the greatest night of the year. Now, let's get to work, shall we?" She spread her wings to fly, then said, "Ooh! Dearie-dearest me, I almost forgot. I have a special task for Treasure." She surveyed the many furry faces, but did not see Treasure. "Has Treasure already left?" she asked. "Was she ever even here, dears?"

"Come to think of it," said Pumpkin, "I haven't seen Treasure all afternoon!"

"Or heard her!" said Berry, moving her ears.

"Where is our Treasure?" Ms. Featherbon said. "I must find her!"

"We'll take a moment to help you!" said Petite.

"Thank you, Palace Pets!" exclaimed Ms. Featherbon. "Let's shake a tail feather!"

As the Critterzens set off to begin their preparations for the Glitter Ball, Ms. Featherbon and the Palace Pets zoomed off to look for Treasure.

"Do you think Treasure's in the Pawlace?" said Ms. Featherbon as they approached the castle.

"*Paw*-sibly!" said Pumpkin.

"Maybe we'll find Dreamy, too!" said Berry.

"Keep your eyes and ears open!"

The pets sped across the gold-tiled bridge leading to the front gates of the Pawlace.

They gathered in the quiet of the **Great Hall**. Sunlight streamed in from the high latticed windows.

"Where do we look first?" asked Berry.

"Let's see . . ." said Petite, flipping through her *Manual of Missing Things*. "According to my manual, there are over nine hundred and two places to lose things in the Pawlace." She put a hoof to her forehead. "This could take all neeeigh-t!"

"Don't panic, dearies," said Ms. Featherbon. "Let's try one place at a time."

"How about we check my kitchen?" said Berry.

"Race you there!" said Sultan.

They all entered **Berry's Kitchen**.

"Treasure!" Berry said. **"Come out, come out, wherever you are!"**

Pumpkin danced across the room. "I don't see her!" said Pumpkin.

Sultan slid under the long wooden table. "She's not under here!" he said.

Petite peeked behind a cart of pies. "Or behind here!" she said.

Ms. Featherbon perched on the chandelier. **"Oh dear, oh dear!"** she cried.

"Oh, my *blues*-berries!" said Berry. "And no sign of Dreamy, either."

"Perk up! My library's where I'd be!" Petite said. "Let's go!" She pranced out of the kitchen. The others followed her through the Pawlace halls until they reached Petite's Library, a large room full of globes and tall shelves stocked with books.

Petite lifted up a plump purple pillow. "Well, she's not under here," she said.

Pumpkin shimmied up a ladder leaning against a bookshelf. "Or up here," she said.

Berry sifted through a tub of apples. "Or in here!" she said. She took a bite out of one. "Yum!"

Sultan dove under a long scroll of paper. "Rawr! Where could she be?" he said.

"Wait a second!" said Pumpkin.

Everyone looked at her.

"We need to *think* like Treasure in order to *find* Treasure," she said. "Where would *she* want to go?"

Petite flipped through her manual titled *How to Think like Treasure*. She pushed her glasses up. "The number one place to find Treasure is Whisker Sea!" she said.

"Of course!" said Ms. Featherbon. "Let's not dally!" She flew out of the Pawlace with the Palace Pets following her.

They **ran** through **Whisker Haven Village** and found themselves on the **beach**.

"Treasure just *has* to be here!" said Berry.

"I'll bet my tickling tiger tail on it!" said Sultan.

"Treasure," Ms. Featherbon sang. "Where's my Treasuuuure?"

Far below, Ms. Featherbon spotted Treasure!

The orange-red kitten with sparkling blue eyes was sailing on her sailboat in the rolling waves of **Whisker Sea**. She was having a grand old time, without a care in Whisker Haven.

"**There you are, dearie!**" said Ms. Featherbon. She swooped down and landed on the bow of Treasure's sailboat.

Treasure smiled. "Ahoy, Ms. Featherbon! Your Treasure is right here! Care to join my crew on the high seas of Whisker Haven?"

The Palace Pets waved at her from the beach.

"We were looking everywhere for you!" called Pumpkin, dancing with joy.

"We should have known you'd be right where you like to be," said Petite with a smile.

"We're happy we found you," said Berry.

"It was a **rawr-some** treasure hunt, that's for sure!" said Sultan.

"Hey, where's Dreamy?" asked Treasure.

"She's off catnapping," said Ms. Featherbon. "She's the next kitten we're going to look for."

"Well, I'm so glad to see you!" said Treasure. "You found me!"

"And we couldn't be happier," said Ms. Featherbon.

Treasure Seeker

"**I**sn't it a paw-fect day to go sailing, **Ms. Featherbon?**" asked Treasure.

The kitten was lying in her sailboat on **Whisker Sea**. The sun was **shining**, and Ms. Featherbon was perched on the bow of Treasure's sailboat wearing a **humdinged expression**.

"It's no time to sail the seas and relax," said Ms. Featherbon. "At least, not yet!"

"**Cartwheeling catfish!**" said Treasure. She bolted upright. "What in whiskers do you mean?"

"Did you forget what today is, my dear?" asked Ms. Featherbon.

"Sailing the Seas Day?" asked Treasure.

"No," said Ms. Featherbon.

"Float Your Boat Day?" asked Treasure.

"It's the day of the Glitter Ball!" said Ms. Featherbon.

Treasure smacked a paw to her forehead and said, "I totally forgot!"

"Dearie-dearest me!" said Ms. Featherbon.

"Oh, Ms. Featherbon, I'm sorry!" said Treasure.

"Have no fear!" said Ms. Featherbon. "I'm glad I found you. The others are all busy preparing, but there's plenty of work to do. I'd love your help, too."

"Sure!" Treasure said, sticking out her paw.

Ms. Featherbon shook it. "Simply marvelous!" she said. "I have a very important task for you. And a very long list of tasks . . . Now if only I can remember . . . Oh, dear." Ms. Featherbon fluttered in circles.

"Ah-ha! I remember! I need my Glitterbits!" she said.

"**I'm on it!**" said Treasure. "Where are your Glitterbits?"

Ms. Featherbon landed on the sailboat and looked left and right. She touched her wing to her beak. She scratched her head. She **mumbled** and **grumbled** and **sighed**.

"Umm . . . Ms. Featherbon?" asked Treasure. "Do you remember where you left your Glitterbits?"

"**Oh, well, ha-ha-ha!** Yes, yes, that's a very good question indeed," said Ms. Featherbon.

Treasure cocked her head to the side.

"I don't know where they are!" Ms. Featherbon exclaimed. "I misplaced them...again!"
"Oh, no!" said Treasure.

"I think they're in the **Pawlace**," said Ms. Featherbon, "but I can't remember where! I need your help or the Glitter Ball will be . . . glitter-less!"

"That's no problem!" said Treasure, standing tall. "Treasure's my middle name!" She paused. "Well, actually, it's my first name. . . . The point is, I'm all about finding treasure!"

And with that, Treasure docked her sailboat on the beach and took off in search of the missing Glitterbits.

"Good luck, dear!" Ms. Featherbon called

after her. "See you at the Glitter Ball this evening!"

"Adventure ahoy!" Treasure raced through the village. She poked her head into Mr. Chow's Kibble Shop, but there were no Glitterbits hiding in the kibbles—only Mr. Chow and Berry doing some taste-testing.

At Lucy's Squeak & Ball Supply Shop, Treasure found Lucy and Sultan digging through bins of squeak balls looking for the best of the best; there were no Glitterbits in there, either.

And finally, at Tillie's Tutu Tailor,

Tillie, Pumpkin, and Petite were decorating fancy outfits. Treasure looked among the tulle, but there were no Glitterbits to be found.

If Treasure didn't find the Glitterbits, everyone's preparations for the ball would be for nothing!

Treasure decided it was time to check the **Pawlace**. She crossed the **long gold-tiled bridge and hustled through the blue iron doors**. Knowing that Ms. Featherbon was always losing things in the most obvious places, Treasure headed through the **Throne Room** toward **Ms. Featherbon's Atrium**. After all, Treasure knew that's where Ms. Featherbon liked to spend quite a bit of her time.

As she passed through the Throne Room, something caught Treasure's eye.

"**Hello?**"
said Treasure.

Stumbling out of Princess Aurora's magical stained glass portal came Dreamy the fluffy pink kitten, who still looked sleepy after her midafternoon nap. In fact, **it seemed like she might be sleepwalking**.

"Must…wake…up." Dreamy yawned. "Must …help…Ms. Featherbon…Glitter Ball." Then she stretched and climbed onto one of the softest pillows in the room. After walking in a few circles, she curled up and **fell asleep**.

Treasure couldn't help smiling at the kitten. "Dream well, Dreamy. I'll make sure to let the others know I found you," she whispered. She tiptoed away toward the hallway but noticed that another four-legged animal—an adorable pink puppy—had also **hopped** out of Princess Aurora's portal.

With curly ears and fluffy hair, the furry little fuzz ball looked as cute, sweet, and dainty as a fairy. The puppy **bounded** across the Throne Room and looked all around at the splendor. Her big bright eyes became even **bigger** and **brighter**.

Seeing Treasure, the puppy said, "Hi there! Have we met? **My name's Macaron.** What's yours?"

"I'm Treasure! Please excuse me. I'm on a very important mission!" said Treasure, leaving the room.

Macaron was right on her tail. "What are we doing?" Macaron asked. "And where are we going?"

Each time Macaron caught up with her, Treasure would sprint ahead. **"Wait!"** Macaron called after her. **"What's going on?"**

Finally, Treasure stopped in front of the birdbath in **Ms. Featherbon's Atrium**, a beautiful room with plants, birdhouses, and a glass-and-gold roof. Ms. Featherbon's birdbath sat in the center and was an enchanting sight to see. It **shimmered** and **glimmered** and **gleamed**.

"I'm looking for Ms. Featherbon's magical Glitterbits!" said Treasure. "And I think they're in here somewhere!"

Upon hearing the word **magical**, Macaron's eyes lit up even more. "I really like magic," she said.

"Is this birdbath magical, too?" asked Macaron with a smile. She jumped right in, splishing and splashing wildly.

"Shimmering seashells!" said Treasure.

Macaron looked around. "Hmmm. So where are the Glitterbits? **I want magic now!**"

Treasure looked around and smiled. Because there, sitting right on the edge of the birdbath, was what Treasure had been seeking. "**Meow-wow! We found them!**" Treasure gestured to Ms. Featherbon's sack of **Glitterbits**, then smiled and said, "Now the Glitter Ball will be all aglitter."

Treasure Lends a Paw

"**A**re Glitterbits extra magical?" asked Macaron.

She and Treasure stood in **Ms. Featherbon's Atrium**, looking at the sack of **Glitterbits** resting on the edge of the birdbath.

"They sure are!" said Treasure. "Let's take them and head over to Whisker Woods. Ms. Featherbon needs the Glitterbits for the **Glitter Ball**."

"What's the . . . Glitter Ball?" asked Macaron.

"The Glitter Ball is a big dance party, where

Glitterworks light up the sky for all the Palace Pets and Critterzens to enjoy as everyone dances and has a *purr*-fect time!" said Treasure.

"Sounds sparkly!" said Macaron. "I love sparkly things! Almost as much as I love magical things!"

"Paw-some! Oh, Ms. Featherbon is going to be so proud of us!" Treasure said with a smile.

"So, who's Ms. Featherbon?" asked Macaron.

"She's our gatekeeper," said Treasure.

"Why does Whisker Haven need a gatekeeper?" asked Macaron.

"To keep out danger and mischief," said Treasure, reaching for the Glitterbits.

"Mischief?" said Macaron. "Mischief is my middle name!" Just then, the fluffy little puppy swooped in and snatched the sack of Glitterbits. She slung it around her body and went sprinting out of the atrium.

Treasure's eyes went wide and she gasped. "Macaron!" she called after her.

"That's Magical Macaron to you!" the puppy called.

"come back here right now!"
Treasure called.

Treasure raced after her, out of the **Pawlace** and into **Whisker Haven Village**.

"Somebody stop that puppy!" Treasure said.

Macaron bolted down the cobblestone street, trying to lose Treasure and accidentally **spilling Glitterbits everywhere**!

Treasure was hot on her tail. She turned a corner, and . . .

The puppy had darted into Mr. Chow's Kibble Shop.

Treasure stopped to catch her breath. "*Meow-*argh!" she said. "If Ms. Featherbon doesn't have her Glitterbits back by tonight, the Glitter Ball can't go on!"

Just then, a voice rang out from Mr. Chow's Kibble Shop. "Stop right there!"

"I smell trouble!" Treasure said. She raced through the shop's open door.

Inside, Macaron had run right around all the bins of kibbles, knocking them aside and sending the kibbles, Mr. Chow, and **Berry** flying.

"Please stop that puppy, Treasure!" said Berry. "She's making a *berry* big mess!"

"Kibblety-gibble, my preparations are a disaster! My poor, poor kibbles!" said Mr. Chow.

His shop looked like it had been turned upside down and shaken like a snow globe. All the special kibbles that Mr. Chow and Berry had sorted and set aside for the Glitter Ball were now spilled across the floor . . . and covered with Glitterbits!

Suddenly, the kibbles, which were enchanted by the Glitterbits, began to hover and float away!

Treasure chased after Macaron. "Please stop!" Treasure called out.

But Macaron just kept on running.

Treasure caught a glimpse of Macaron disappearing into Lucy's shop.

"Oh, no! Not the **Squeak and Ball Supply Shop**!" said Treasure. She raced inside as fast as she could.

"Watch out!" called Sultan.

Treasure ducked to avoid a **flying squeak ball**.

Lucy and **Sultan** also dodged this way and that. Macaron had showered Glitterbits everywhere, and now the balls were zooming around the shop!

"*Meow*-arrgh! This is terrible!" said Treasure as she looked around at the chaos. There was no Macaron in sight. "Where did that pink puppy go?" she asked.

Lucy and Sultan pointed out the door.

"She went that way!" said Sultan.

Treasure bounded outside. She saw Macaron's pink tail vanishing into Tillie's Tutu Tailor.

67

"No! Not the tutus, too!" cried Treasure.

Treasure hurried into the shop. There, she bumped right into **Tillie**, Pumpkin, and Petite, who were looking up at the ceiling. Treasure looked up, too, and saw enchanted tutus whirling in the air!

"Did a persistent pink puppy do this?" asked Treasure.

"Yes!" said Tillie. **"If we don't get those twirling tutus down, we won't have any outfits for the Glitter Ball!"**

Suddenly, the dancing tutus **swooped down** and **flew right out the door**!

"Oh, no! My tutus!" shouted Tillie.

"This is tutu-terrible!" added Pumpkin.

"What is that puppy thinking?" asked Petite.

"I'm not sure, but I'll find out!" said Treasure.

Treasure ran outside with Pumpkin, Petite, and Tillie following close behind. There, they saw the most amazing thing—**tutus**, **squeak balls**, and **kibbles** were flying across the sky.

"What about the Glitter Ball?" asked Lucy.

"We can't have it without kibbles!" said a sad Mr. Chow, stepping out from his kibble shop.

The enchanted items whizzed through the air just as Jane Hair stepped out of her salon. She held a hand mirror and smiled at her reflection.

"Oh, yes! My hairstyle for the Glitter Ball looks molto bene!" Jane Hair announced.

Just as Jane admired her hair, **squeak balls, tutus, and kibbles came flying at her**!

"Ah! My hair! Help!" called Jane.

"Hold on, I'll help you!" shouted Treasure.

Treasure jumped up and batted away the enchanted items. But as she saved Jane from a bad hair day, Treasure accidentally sent everything flying up **even higher** in the air!

"Come back!" cried Treasure.

"I've been working on my hair for the Glitter Ball all day long," said Jane Hair. "If you hadn't helped me, it would have been ruined. Grazie!"

"You're welcome, Jane," said Treasure. "But I'm afraid the Glitter Ball won't happen if I don't get those Glitterbits back from that puppy!"

"No Glitter Ball? But what about my fancy hair?" asked Jane Hair, clasping her paws.

"Don't worry, I'll do my best to make sure you get to show off your fancy hair at the ball, Jane," said Treasure.

"Can I help?" asked Jane Hair.

"Yes! You all can!" said Treasure, looking at the Critterzens who had joined together.

"Do everything you can to help Ms. Featherbon with the Glitter Ball. And I'll try to find those Glitterbits," said Treasure. "Now, who saw where that puppy ran off to?" she asked.

"The trail of Glitterbits seems to be heading

toward the **beach**," said Mr. Chow.

Treasure looked. Mr. Chow was right. **Macaron had left a trail of Glitterbits going right for the shore!**

"I'm going to get those Glitterbits so the ball can go on," said Treasure.

"**Good luck!**" her friends cheered.

"I promised Ms. Featherbon I'd lend a paw, and that's exactly what I plan to do," said Treasure.

Treasure raced off to the beach. "Macaron!" she shouted. "I need those Glitterbits!"

Treasure Sets Sail

Treasure had followed Macaron's **trail of Glitterbits** all the way to the **beach**.

There, Treasure spotted her, sitting in the sand and wearing one of Tillie's Glitter Ball tutus.

"Macaron!" Treasure yelled.

The puppy spun around. "Who, me?" she said.

"Yes, YOU!" Treasure said. "You ruined all the Glitter Ball preparations!"

"I did?" asked Macaron.

"We still might be able to save the Glitter Ball,"

said Treasure. "Would you please give me the Glitterbits?"

"Oh! You want the Glitterbits?" Macaron grabbed the sack and shook it.

"Yes, I want the Glitterbits!" said Treasure. "Please give them back to me."

"You have to say the magic words!" Macaron said through her teeth, with a sly smile.

"I said *please*," said Treasure. "Now paw it over. Ms. Featherbon is relying on me!"

"If you want them back, you're going to have to catch me!" Macaron bolted down the beach.

"This is a *cat*-astrophe!" Treasure said. "Stop! This isn't a game!" Treasure raced after the puppy. "Oh, you're going to be very sorry you swiped the Glitterbits. . . . Just as soon . . . as I . . . catch you!" Treasure picked up speed, sending sand flying in her wake.

When Macaron jumped over a piece of driftwood, Treasure followed, clearing the wood.

"Stop right there!" Treasure said.

Macaron dove onto her belly to get under a leafy sea shrub ahead of them. Treasure slid under all the twisted branches and made it to the other side.

"I hope you like mud!" Macaron shouted.

"Huh?" said Treasure.

Macaron leaped over a puddle of sandy mud.

"A little mud isn't going to stop me!" said Treasure. "Hearts! Hooves! Paws!" She bounded into the muck.

By the time Treasure got to the other side of the

sandy mud puddle, **Macaron had hopped into Treasure's sailboat**, which had been resting on the beach. She pushed off, and the sailboat glided out across the water.

Treasure didn't have much time. "Stop right there! Please, come back!"

Macaron stuck out her tongue at Treasure. She continued to sail farther and farther away.

The Glitterbits floated
out of the sack, leaving a
sparkling trail in the sky.

"Too bad cats hate water!" said Macaron, laughing.

"Not this cat!" said Treasure. She jumped right into the water and started swimming out to catch Macaron.

Macaron had a good lead on her, but the sea was Treasure's playground. "When it comes to navigating waves, no one is better than me!" Treasure said, paddling faster.

By that time, Macaron was trying to outsail her, steering the sailboat and catching a nice big gust of wind. But when she turned around to see how much distance she had from Treasure, Treasure was hopping into the sailboat.

As Treasure grabbed the sack of Glitterbits, Macaron yelped, "Bow-wow-ow!"

"Paws off!" said Treasure.

But Macaron wasn't yet ready to give up. She snapped her teeth on the other side of the sack, leading to a big **tug-of-war**. But Treasure battled for the sack with her whole heart and two strong paws and finally managed to take it from the puppy.

"Me-wow!" Treasure said. "Now I'm going to return the Glitterbits to Ms. Featherbon so she can kick off the Glitter Ball."

"Ooh! The Glitter Ball! Let's go!" said Macaron.

"We'll go," Treasure said, "but first you have to tell me why you took Ms. Featherbon's Glitterbits."

"Because I love anything having to do with magic!" Macaron said. "I've always dreamed of having magic. When I heard that the Glitterbits were magical, I just had to have them."

"Who doesn't want to have magic?" said Treasure. "But you didn't have to swipe them from me."

"I'm sorry," said Macaron. "Can you ever forgive me for ruining all the preparations and for taking you on a wild goose chase?"

Treasure smiled. "Don't you mean a wild puppy chase?" she said.

Macaron giggled.

"A-paw-logy accepted!" said Treasure. "But your behavior doesn't fit with the royal heart of friendship code of the Palace Pets. When we go to the Glitter Ball, you should say you're sorry to all the nice Critterzens for the glitter chaos you've caused throughout Whisker Haven."

"I promise," said Macaron.

Treasure put her paw out to Macaron, and the puppy put hers on top. "Hearts! Hooves! Paws!" Treasure said.

"Hearts! Hooves! Paws!" said Macaron, with a smile. "And magic!"

Treasure Sparkles

"Have you always been paw-struck by magic?" Treasure asked Macaron.

"Have I ever!" said the little pink puppy. She and Treasure sailed toward the shore, with Treasure steering the sailboat. "Don't tell, but I once tried to swipe a magic wand from three good fairies!"

"Oh, my fish biscuits!" said Treasure.

"But that didn't work out so well . . ." Macaron said. "Can you imagine what it would have been like?" She took the sack of Glitterbits and held it up with one paw. With the other, she pretended she was holding a wand. "You just wave the wand like this." She mimed waving her imaginary wand over the sack of sparkling, magical Glitterbits. "Then you say a magic spell like 'Bibbidi-bobbidi—'"

But just then, some of the Glitterbits tickled Macaron's nose.

Macaron sneezed.

"Achoooooooooooo!"

The sneeze rocked Macaron's body. She released her grip on the sack of Glitterbits. In one split second, the sack of Ms. Featherbon's magical Glitterbits—**the very Glitterbits** needed for the Glitter Ball that night—fell from her paws, **sending Glitterbits into the sea.**

"Meow-no!" Treasure said. She grabbed a fishing net on a pole and tried to save the Glitterbits from the water. But the holes in her net made it impossible to catch them, and the Glitterbits disappeared into the sea. Treasure put down the fishing net and covered her eyes with her paws.

"Meow-aaarrrrgh! Now the Glitter Ball has lost its sparkle for good! What in whiskers will we do?" she said.

Macaron's jaw dropped. "Treasure, I am so, so, *so* sorry!" she said. "This is all my fault. I feel terrible that **I've ruined the Glitter Ball**."

But suddenly, the sea started to stir. The Glitterbits in the water created a whirlpool. **It sent Treasure's sailboat spinning!**

"Oh, no!" said Treasure. She held on to the sailboat tightly with her paws.

Macaron did the same.

The whirlpool spit them out, **sending the sailboat flying to the shore**.

Treasure and Macaron landed with a *THUD* and got up, their fur soggy and their spirits dampened.

"So what are we going to do now?" asked Macaron.

"Good question," said Treasure. "Maybe we should tell the truth."

"I'm scared," said Macaron. "Won't all your friends be mad at us?"

"It's okay," said Treasure. "They'll forgive us."

Macaron sighed and said, "Okay."

"Let's go," said Treasure.

As the sun set, Treasure and Macaron headed to Whisker Woods to deliver the bad news to everyone. There were strings of **lights** and **lanterns** in **Whisker Haven Village** leading to **Whisker Woods**.

Treasure said, "Everything looks . . ."

"Magical!" said Macaron.

Treasure and Macaron walked down the path and entered the clearing in Whisker Woods, which had a few **lights**, **streamers**, **balloons**, and a table with a single pie. The **Palace Pets** and

Critterzens were all there and dressed in their normal, everyday outfits.

Taken aback by their lackluster and ordinary surroundings, Treasure and Macaron couldn't help wincing.

As Treasure glanced around at the not-so-splendificent Glitter Ball, she saw someone coming her way: Ms. Featherbon!

"**Treasure!**" Ms. Featherbon chirped. "**I'm so glad to see you!**"

"*Me*-ow, too!" said Treasure.

Ms. Featherbon flew over the clearing and sang a ditty: "We've all worked hard, we've all chipped in! And now the Glitter Ball can finally begin!" She settled on a tree branch and looked around. "Oh, dear! Where are all the Glitter Ball kibbles, squeak balls, and tutus?" she asked.

Treasure gulped and glanced at Macaron. She thought about how everything had flown away. . . .

"Oh, no matter!" said Ms. Featherbon. "At least I can set off the Glitterworks and sprinkle Glitterbits

on everything so that this Glitter Ball can shine. But Treasure, dear ... **where are my Glitterbits?**"

"Me-uh . . . me-er . . ." Treasure said. "Your Glitterbits . . . right." She heaved a deep sigh and glanced around.

Everyone looked at Treasure. It grew **quiet**. A cricket chirped.

The cricket, feeling all eyes on it, said, "Oops. Sorry."

"Well, Ms. Featherbon," Treasure said. "I have good news . . . and bad news."

"Start with the good!" Ms. Featherbon said. "Always, always start with the good!"

"Okay, well, the good news is that I met a new friend today," said Treasure.

"I'm Macaron," said the puppy. "Like the dessert."

"Well, isn't that splendificently delightful!" Ms. Featherbon said. "What's the bad news, dear? I'm sure it's not so bad."

Treasure looked at Macaron, who stood there, frozen. Then she looked back at Ms. Featherbon. "The bad news . . ." Treasure began.

"Yes?" said Ms. Featherbon. "What is it, Treasure?"

Treasure **gulped** and took a deep breath. What could she possibly say?

"I just wanted to say . . ." said Treasure. "I don't have your Glitterbits." Treasure's eyes shimmered with tears. "And I'm sorry. I hope I didn't ruin the Glitter Ball."

Macaron stepped forward. "Umm . . . Ms. Featherbon, I have something to tell you, too," she said.

"Yes, Macaron? What is it?" asked Ms. Featherbon.

"Treasure did everything right. I was the one who did everything wrong."

"It's her!" called Mr. Chow. "The puppy who made a Glitterbit mess of Whisker Haven!"

The Critterzens grumbled.

"Quiet down, please, everyone," said Ms. Featherbon. **"Macaron, dear, I'm not sure I understand what you mean."**

"You see, I swiped your Glitterbits. Then I ran amok all through Whisker Haven when Treasure started chasing me. It's my fault that the preparations went flying off. I'm so sorry for my inconsiderate behavior. I just wanted to do magic so desperately that I forgot about others."

"Truly?" asked Ms. Featherbon.

Macaron nodded. "If I hadn't taken the remaining Glitterbits out on Treasure's sailboat, then I would have never sneezed them into the sea!" Macaron's head drooped. "I'm sorry!"

"Oh, dearie-dearest me!" Ms. Featherbon said. "This is all very unexpected!"

Macaron looked out at the Critterzens. "And I'm so sorry I made a mess of your things," she said.

"**We forgive you,**" said Lucy.

The other Critterzens nodded.

"She's learned her lesson," said Ms. Featherbon.

Macaron nodded. "I just wish I hadn't ruined the Glitter Ball in the process," she said.

Ms. Featherbon smiled. "Chin up, pup! Now, everyone, I want you all to follow me. I think this Glitter Ball can be saved after all!"

Ms. Featherbon flew out of **Whisker Woods**, away from the clearing.

Treasure and the rest of the Palace Pets and Critterzens followed her onto the **beach**.

"Let's get this party started!" Ms. Featherbon said. She flew over the water. "First thing's first," said Ms. Featherbon. She extended her wings and fluttered them. As she did, something splendificent happened!

Piece by piece and bit by bit, all the kibbles and squeak balls and tutus that the Palace Pets and Critterzens had spent all day preparing for the Glitter Ball magically flew onto the beach.

Then, with a wave of Ms. Featherbon's wings, the Glitterbits that had sunk to the bottom of the sea magically rose out of the water and floated into the sky.

"Hearts! Hooves! Paws!" shouted Treasure.

Then the Glitterbits launched into the sky above the beach and formed Glitterworks in the shapes of hearts, hooves, and paws.

"Paw-fect!" exclaimed Treasure.

Looking at her wingy-work, Ms. Featherbon smiled.

After much **oohing** and **aahing** from the crowd, the Glitterbits fell, showering down on everyone lucky enough to be there. Macaron was absolutely amazed by the fantastic display of magic.

"Look at me!" Dreamy said. "It's like I'm . . . dreaming."

"Hi, Dreamy!" said Treasure. "I'm glad you could make it to the Glitter Ball!"

Dreamy yawned. "Me . . . too . . ." she said.

"Isn't tonight just paw-fect now?" Pumpkin danced a little jig on the beach.

Sultan dove into a glitter pile. "Rawr-some!" he said.

"What a berry lovely evening!" said Berry, hopping up and down in delight.

Petite looked up from her Glitter Ball manual. "Things aren't going according to plan," she said. She tossed her book aside. "But that's okay!" She danced alongside her friends.

"The Glitter Ball is saved!"
said Treasure.

Soon all the Palace Pets and Critterzens were covered in Glitterbits, and their fur shimmered and glimmered in the evening light.

Treasure looked down. She sparkled.

"What a purr-fect Glitter Ball this turned out to be," said Treasure. Then she looked at Ms. Featherbon, who was flitting through the sky. "Thank you!" she said.

As **Lily** the jazzy purple kitten started up her band with **trumpets** and **horns**, Ms. Featherbon

watched everyone break into dance. She knew that **everybody had come together** to help create a **very special night** indeed. With her own work behind her, **it was time for Ms. Featherbon to enjoy the party, too.** She swooped down beside Treasure and Macaron on the sand.

"**Treasure,**" she said, "now it's my turn to thank you for all the hard work you've done today in trying to find and track down my beloved Glitterbits. **The Glitter Ball wouldn't have been**

the same without you, and thank you for being honest with me." She turned to Macaron. "And you, too, Macaron. *You're as sweet as your name implies.*"

Macaron smiled.

So did Treasure.

"Sparkle away, my dears," said Ms. Featherbon.

Treasure's smile grew wider. **"I was happy to help,"** Treasure said. "But I couldn't have done it without **the royal heart of friendship**." Catching Macaron's eye, Treasure gave her a wink. And her new dear friend Macaron winked back.

Good-bye for now!

Sailboat Instructions

Step 1: Pop out all of the sailboat pieces.

Step 2: Insert all of the pieces into the sailboat bottom by matching the letters on the pieces with the letters on the sailboat bottom. *Paw*-fect!

Step 3: Place Treasure inside of the sailboat and set sail for adventure!